THE TORTOISE AND THE SOLDIER

THE
TORTOISE
AND THE
SOLDIER

Based on True Events

•

MICHAEL FOREMAN

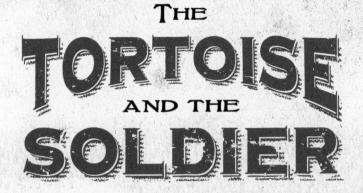

HENRY HOLT AND COMPANY
NEW YORK

Henry Holt and Company, LLC
Publishers since 1866
175 Fifth Avenue, New York, New York 10010
mackids.com

Library of Congress Cataloging-in-Publication Data
Foreman, Michael, 1938–
The tortoise and the soldier : a story of courage and friendship in World War I / Michael Foreman.
     pages   cm
     ISBN 978-1-62779-173-1 (hardback) — ISBN 978-1-62779-174-8 (e-book)
   1. Foreman, Michael, 1938– —Childhood and youth. 2. World War, 1914–1918—
     Great Britain—Biography. 3. Illustrators—Great Britain—Biography.
       4. Authors, English—20th century—Biography. I. Title.
     PR6056.O675Z46 2015   741.6092—dc23 [B]   2014047282

Henry Holt books may be purchased for business or promotional use. For information on
bulk purchases, please contact the Macmillan Corporate and Premium Sales Department at
(800) 221-7945 x5442 or by e-mail at specialmarkets@macmillan.com.

Originally published by Templar Publishing in the United Kingdom in 2013
First American edition—2015 / Designed by Meredith Pratt
Printed in China by RR Donnelley Asia Printing Solutions Ltd., Dongguan City, Guangdong Province

1 3 5 7 9 10 8 6 4 2

◆ IN FOND MEMORY OF ◆

Henry Friston
and with much gratitude to his son Don
for a lifetime's friendship
and for sharing his father's story

THE
TORTOISE
AND THE
SOLDIER

ONE

IT WAS THE 1950S, and I was working for the local paper, the *Lowestoft Journal*. I told my mates I was a junior reporter, but really, I was just the office boy. Now and again I'd be trusted with a reporting job. Small jobs only, mind. And only when the proper reporters were busy. Still, it got me out of the office and away from the endless filing and tea runs.

It was weddings mainly. Everyone got married on a Saturday back then, so there was often a big fancy do at the church and a small wedding in the chapel at the same time. You can probably guess which one I got to report on.

I used to be given other stories too, the ones that

seemed to come round again and again, just like the seasons. Summer would mean the village fete, where old Fred Carver always won the competition for Most Impressive Vegetable (thanks to the ready supply of horse manure that came from the blacksmith's next door). Autumn, it'd be the church harvest festival, then winter was the school Christmas party. Just the names and dates needed changing and—Bob's your uncle—there was my report.

But when it came to spring, well, there was one story that meant spring had well and truly sprung . . . and I'd never been given the chance to report on it: Henry Friston and his famous tortoise.

It was a grayish morning in March, when the editor yelled to me across the newsroom, "Say, Trev, pop along and check on Mr. Friston's tortoise, would you? See if it's awake yet."

Back in those days, normal folk didn't have telephones at home. So, with my reporter's pad and some freshly sharpened pencils in my top pocket (I always wrote in pencil so I could check my spelling before I handed in my report), I jumped on my rusty old bike and pedaled off to the tiny village of Corton.

It was Corton where Mr. Henry Friston (age fifty-nine) lived, in a pair of restored railway carriages, with his family and his tortoise, Ali Pasha (age sixty-eight-ish).

Mr. Friston was digging in his garden when I wobbled up the lane.

"Aha!" he said, catching sight of me and my pocketful of pencils. "The *Journal*, is it? Well, you're bang on time;

Ali Pasha woke up this weekend just gone." Henry pointed to a small wooden box sitting in a pool of sunshine, next to a rain barrel.

"He's not living outside yet," the old man continued. "It's still a bit too cold at night. But he does like a spot of sunshine."

I propped up my ancient bike and squatted down

next to the wooden box. The tortoise didn't look too pleased to see me, but I was enchanted by his crinkly, beaky head and the wise old eyes that blinked beadily in my direction. I'd never seen a real live tortoise before.

"Why is he called Ali Pasha?" I blurted out.

Not the finest opening question, I know.

"It's a very long story," said Henry. "Too long to go into now." My face must have fallen, but Henry, with a twinkle in his eye, continued, "If you're really interested, come back at the weekend, and I can tell you more. Sundays are best."

So I climbed on my bike and weaved my wonky way back to the office. I told the assistant editor that Ali Pasha was indeed awake, a photographer was sent off to take a picture, and the usual report went into Friday's paper, under the headline ALI'S AWAKE—SPRING HAS SPRUNG!

But I knew there was more to this story. And I couldn't wait to find out what that was.

TWO

Sunday came and, pencils in pocket, I headed off to Corton on my rusty steed. I'd spent so much of Saturday trying to come up with questions a proper reporter might ask that I'd hardly had time to eat, and my mum had started fussing that I was sickening for something. But I knew there was a story waiting to be discovered, a proper story, and I was determined to be the one to get it.

When I arrived at the railway carriage, Henry was busy in the garden again. "Hello, young fella," he said. "Brought your pencils, I see."

Henry stuck his fork into the earth and beckoned me toward a weather-beaten garden bench. Ali's wooden box was on the ground beside it.

"Take a seat. The wife's out helping at Sunday school this morning, so we shan't be disturbed. Would you like some apple juice?"

I'd never had juice quite like it. The deliciously crisp taste cleared my head of all the jumbled-up questions that were whizzing around in there. I told Henry so.

"Well, old Ali loves an apple, let me tell you." Henry sat down beside me on the bench and lifted the tortoise gently out of the box and onto his lap. "Goes back to our time in Egypt. . . ."

And with that, Henry Friston began to tell me his story.

★　　★　　★　　★

It all started with a map. This map was pinned to the schoolroom wall, and it had all the countries of the world on it. So many places, in fact, that it was difficult to believe they were all out there somewhere, just waiting to be explored. They were called things like Zanzibar and Honolulu, and, well, names like that are exciting enough to make any young lad's mind wander, aren't they? My mind was no different. I'd just stare at that map, with its mountains and deserts and wide expanses of pale blue sea, and I'd daydream. . . .

Until Miss Hood threw a piece of chalk at my head to snap me out of it—which happened quite a lot.

"Daydreaming will get you no-where, Henry Friston!" she would squawk, like an angry seagull, and send me to stand in the corner.

But I didn't mind. When I stood in the corner and faced the wall, I could carry on daydreaming in peace!

Sometimes, Miss Hood would keep me late to catch up on the lesson. I didn't mind this either— the classroom was quiet and peaceful, and Miss Hood was less fierce after school. She would

look up from her marking and study me over the rim of her spectacles, like I was a tricky sum she was trying to solve.

"You're a bright boy, Henry Friston," she said to me on one such occasion, after I'd spent the entire morning watching a dragonfly zooming around outside. "But you're such a dreamer. Dreams are all well and good, but you need a plan, or they will never come true."

I decided then that Miss Hood was more like a wise old owl than an angry seagull.

When I was thirteen, I left school, as a lot of other

boys did at the time. My family lived at the entrance to the local country estate—me; my parents; grandparents; my brothers, Ernest and Arthur; and my sisters, Ethel and Hilda, all crammed together into a tiny cottage with tall chimneys called Hawthorn Lodge. My dad worked as head gardener at the Big House on the cliffs, and my ma and grandma were in service there too. So after leaving school, I went and worked with my dad.

I was a proper country boy and loved working outside, tending to the hedges, weeding the flower beds, planting vegetables—anything that kept me out in the fresh air, really. But the Big House also had greenhouses for growing fruit. I didn't often willingly swap the outdoors to work inside, but going into those little glass buildings felt like stepping into another country, one that was hot and far away.

I looked after the melons and grapefruit—they were truly exotic fare back then. Seeing these strange and wonderful fruits ripening in the heat of the greenhouses made me daydream about where they came from. I would wonder whether it was those countries on the schoolroom map that also had strange and wonderful names.

Then, on my fourteenth birthday, I came one step closer to exploring the world. I was offered a job as a deckhand on a steam drifter, The Girl Ena, and swapped a life at the Big House for a life on the ocean wave. It felt like coming home, I tell you. Hauling nets was backbreaking work, and conditions were often rough and cold, but it didn't matter a jot to me. I was riding the rolling North Sea, and the waters stretched out before me as far as the eye could behold, leading to all those countries I had dreamed about.

Oh, yes, I may not have been a schoolboy anymore, but I'd never stopped daydreaming. Although now it wasn't Miss Hood's sticks of chalk that bounced off my head—it was herrings thrown by my crewmates.

I worked on The Girl Ena *for five salty years. But on the twelfth of August, 1913, I got fed up with only dipping my toe in the ocean of adventure and decided it was time to dive right in.*

I joined the Royal Navy.

★ ★ ★ ★

Henry was swaying from side to side slightly as he spoke. I wondered if he was back on that steam drifter right then, still riding the waves in his imagination, still daydreaming, even now. A proper reporter would have been scribbling away furiously as Henry told his story, but I just wanted to listen and watch as the old man spoke, his eyes somewhere far away and his left hand resting protectively on the grizzled shell of his ancient companion.

A few moments of silence ticked awkwardly by, then Henry gave a little shiver and surfaced from his daydream. "Tea?" he asked, carefully lowering Ali back into the wooden box and getting to his feet. "How d'you take it?"

"Just milk, thanks," I said as he disappeared into the nearer of the railway carriages. I looked down at Ali Pasha. The tortoise looked back up at me, blinking. "So, Ali. Want to give me a quote about your pal Henry?" I said to him.

Blink.

"How about telling me what's coming next, then?"

Blink.

"Not exactly front-page stuff, Ali." I chuckled.

Before long, Henry emerged back out into the garden, carrying a tea tray. As he set it down, I noticed there was also a small wooden casket and an old photo on the tray. Henry passed me the photo and sat back as I studied it. It looked like a picture of him, but as I imagined a proper reporter might, I flipped the photo over to see if it had anything written on the back, to be sure. But instead of a name or date, there was just a sequence of letters and numbers: SS4384.

"Is this you, Henry?" I asked. "What does SS4384 mean?"

"Handsome fella, don't you think?" Henry chuckled, and took up the story again.

★ ★ ★ ★

You never forget your navy number, and mine was SS4384. Soon as I got it, they sent me off to the HMS Pembroke base to train to be an ordinary seaman. No amount of hauling nets and landing catches on The Girl Ena *could have prepared me for the right-to-the-bones exhaustion of training—day after day of orders yelled right into your face, endless marches with heavy packs, and tough physical training in all weathers. It was only when I proved myself nifty with a rifle (my dad had taught me to shoot from an early age) that the instructors eased off me a little. It was a blessed relief, that's for sure.*

Eventually, through blood, sweat, and a lot of shots on target at the practice range, I was promoted to able seaman and sent to the battleship HMS Implacable. *First time I clapped eyes on her, I was speechless. I'd seen all sorts of ships when I was out at sea, but none quite as vast as this one. She was like an iron giant. They wanted to train me to fire her enormous guns, and looking at them, I imagined I'd be able to hit the stars with a single shot.*

Life aboard the battleship was like living in a world made entirely of metal. Iron decks, iron walls, iron doors, iron ladders, iron walkways—there was iron everywhere. I was one of a crew of 780, all crammed into small spaces

that smelled of engine oil, coal, sweat, and fried onions from the mess decks. The sheer number of us meant we had to share hammocks at night. As one sailor got up for his spell of duty, his shipmate would swing himself up into the vacated hammock and get his kip. One in; one out. Each night, I'd drop into one of the hammocks like a lead weight and fall into an instant, exhausted sleep, oblivious to the snores and farts of my fellow crew around me.

Number Two Gun belonged to me and my mates—Matt the Cornishman, Long John from Liverpool, and Gus the Scot. All ex-fishermen and all a bit older than me, but we made quite some team. Passing, loading, and punching the heavy shells into the mouth of the great gun was tricky, especially when you were fighting against the rise and fall of the waves out at sea. The slightest slip could result in broken fingers, or worse. You had to trust your team, and I did—I trusted them with my life.

★ ★ ★ ★

Henry leaned over to the tea tray and picked up the small wooden casket that was sitting on it. From his box on the ground, Ali Pasha stretched out his wrinkly neck, as if to get a better view of what was going on.

"This here's my ditty box, lad," Henry said, lifting the lid. "We all got given one on board, to hold our personal possessions and the like."

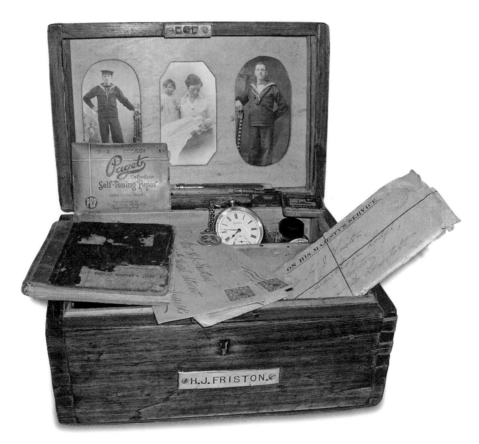

The ditty box was old, but it gleamed from regular polishing and was obviously a treasured possession. As Henry rummaged inside, I got a glimpse of some yellowing postcards and more photographs. I opened my mouth to ask if I could have a look at them, but Henry found what he was looking for and closed the lid. "You can see those another time," he said, answering my unasked question. Instead, he handed me a small, very worn book. It was a dull kind of red with a battered yellow spine, and once again his navy number, SS4384, was written on the cover.

And heaving himself up to standing, Henry headed off to the vegetable patch. I looked at Ali. He looked back. I could have sworn he bobbed his head, just a little, like he was nodding his approval. So I opened the book and discovered brittle pages filled with tight lines of inky script, sometimes introduced by neatly written dates.

It was Henry's wartime diary.

4th August 1914

Would you know it—we're at war with Germany! The quartermaster piped it through when we were coaling the ship around six P.M. this evening. "Hostilities will commence at midnight," he said. Finally looks like we'll get to see some action. About time too.

Wonder where we'll be sent? Wouldn't mind going to Zanzibar. I can still remember exactly where it was on the old school map.

31st October 1914

Well, it's not exactly Zanzibar, but we've made it as far as Belgium. I've been here before, on <u>The Girl Ena</u>, but at least I'm not hauling fish this time. We're landing heavy fire on the Germans ("Fritz," Long John calls them). We're shelling them as they make their way to the Front in France. KABOOOOM!

I heard on the mess deck yesterday that Austria

and Hungary have joined up with the Germans to fight against us. One of the mess boys, Moby Richards—who'd heard it from one of the lads in the telegraph room—told me so as he dolloped a mountain of mash onto my plate. Didn't taste so good after I heard that. Got a little side order of news with my beef broth tonight too—the bloomin' Turks are against us as well. No idea why they're choosing Fritz over us. Hasn't anyone told them the Germans don't have a chance?

Can't help thinking about Ernie and Arthur. They are my kid brothers, after all. Last I heard, they were in France with the army, stuck in no-man's-land. Ma must be going out of her mind with worry, with all three of us away fighting. Bet she's proud of us all, though.

As I read this entry, sitting in the peaceful safety of Henry's garden, I felt a little shiver run up my spine. I had a little brother too. Georgie. I could imagine how worried I'd be if he were out fighting somewhere, miles and miles from home, maybe alive, maybe dead. George could barely fire a decent shot from a catapult, let alone a gun. If this had been wartime, though, he'd have had only a couple more years before call-up. Then he'd have had to go off and fight for his country. And I would have already been at war! How had Henry coped so far from home and so far from news of his family?

I stood up to get a better view of the vegetable patch, but Henry was still bent over his spade, digging and turning the soil. So I sank back down on the bench and carried on reading.

It soon became clear that life on the *Implacable* in Belgium consisted of eating, training, shelling, sleeping, and then shelling some more. Although I'd never have said as much to Henry, I found it all a tiny bit disappointing. Where were the battles, the secret

missions, the daring nighttime raids on enemy territory?
The sailors must have been itching to see some action
after doing the same thing day after day after day—I was
certainly itching to read about it!

I was ready to make a polite excuse to leave, but as

I gently laid the diary on the bench beside me, a sudden gust of wind caught the thin pages and flipped them to the entry for March 13, 1915. I knew instantly that something had changed.

It said just two words: *To Gallipoli!*

THREE

"**WHERE'S GALLIPOLI?**" I called over to Henry.

The old man straightened abruptly from his digging, as if I'd shouted BOO in his ear. He paused for a second, then, pushing his spade into the earth, he headed back to the bench and settled down next to me with a sigh.

"You're not the first to ask me that, you know," he said, the faraway look returning to his eyes. I knew he was back on the *Implacable* again.

I waited as Henry lifted Ali out of his box, settled the tortoise gently into his lap, and began to speak.

★ ★ ★ ★

Cornish Matt asked me the same question forty years ago.

The lads of Number Two Gun always came to me to find out about places they'd heard news of from the telegraph room. They knew I could answer their questions, but I could show them too, thanks to the world map I kept tucked inside my ditty box. My dad had given it to me before I left for war.

"Turkey," I told Cornish Matt. "Gallipoli's the back door to Turkey. We're going to bash in the Turks' back door and give Fritz a little surprise. . . ."

At eight P.M. that night, Implacable and her sister ship, HMS Queen, silently slipped moorings and glided into the Atlantic. Nobody knew the reason we were heading to our destination. It was to be a secret mission, a vital one that could help shorten this war.

We were sailing under sealed orders, which meant that even our commanding officer was in the dark about exactly what we'd be expected to do when we got there, and it was only when we were well onto the high seas that he was allowed to open the envelope containing our instructions. But as always, the news soon leaked through the iron decks of the ship till it reached us able seamen down below.

Four days later, we spotted our first port of call, the

looming shape of the Rock of Gibraltar. It was a sight for sore eyes, I can tell you. After four days of endless drills, we were desperate for a break from both the practice and the choppy seas. But Mother Nature wasn't on our side, and the weather took a turn for the worse. We were forced to carry on, steaming through the Straits of Gibraltar and into the Mediterranean without stopping.

At that moment, I should have felt despondent. Or even afraid. We must have loaded and reloaded Number Two Gun several hundred times over the previous four days, in preparation for the battle that lay ahead. Instead, something happened that made my heart swoop a bit like the butterflies that danced in the summer skies back home. I looked to the starboard bow, and I saw Africa. I SAW AFRICA! Finally, my classroom daydreams were coming true, and I could forget, just for a moment, where I was and what I was heading into.

But had I known, as I fixed my eyes on that magical shoreline, the grim news that was waiting for us in Malta, our next destination, I might not have felt so happy: three British battleships had been blown to smithereens near Gallipoli, and HMS Implacable would be arriving in that very place in just a couple of days' time.

The chatter on the mess deck was subdued that night, but the story went that hundreds and hundreds of sailors had been killed, as well as a ship's cat, Togo. According to Moby, one brave stoker, William Burrows, had tried to save Togo, but he and the cat had both drowned.

All of the Number Two Gunners were now filled with a grim new resolve.

"We'll be there ourselves soon," said Gus. "Let's do it for those poor lads."

"And the cat," I said.

★   ★   ★   ★

Henry's eyes had filled with tears. It was almost as if Ali Pasha sensed his old chum was upset, as he stretched out his bunched-up neck and gave a sad little sigh.

I stood awkwardly, unsure if I should leave Henry to his memories. He looked up briefly as I packed away my pad and pencils, and wiped a callused hand over his eyes. "Hay fever's always worst this time of year," he said gruffly. "You don't have to leave on my account, son. Stay, have another look at that diary of mine. I'll just go and find myself a clean hanky and then I'll put us on another pot of tea."

It shook me up a bit, seeing a grown man cry. I'd only ever seen my dad cry once, and that was when our old dog had to be put to sleep. Henry must have witnessed some truly terrible things in the war.

I opened his diary a little more respectfully and, if I'm honest, a little more nervously too, for I had no idea what stories would emerge next from its yellowing pages.

24th April 1915

Sorry, my dear old diary, I've neglected you this past month. A poor excuse, I know, but I've been a little busy showing Fritz what for....

One thing's for certain—this isn't a drill anymore. We've made it to Gallipoli, and we're loading and firing for real now. The Turks are hiding out in trenches on the cliffs and the headland, and we've got to take out their guns before they get a chance to use them. I swear to you, when all of our battleships are firing, it's as if the sky itself shakes so hard it could just about cave right in.

Now and again, we have to switch from shelling the shore to shelling the sky. The enemy fighter planes are rickety old things and could probably be brought down by one of my homemade catapults—Lord, even a shot from our Ernie could probably bring one down! But those planes come out of nowhere, and the boys on deck have to have their wits about them to have any chance of hitting one.

Some clever bloke back home has come up with a great trick, though! We've got a whole other fleet of battleships that hang about on the horizon, patrolling and, hopefully, putting the wind up the enemy. Only, according to Moby Richards, they're not real battleships. They're just cargo vessels with fake funnels and guns. Ha! Take that, Fritz.

I need to go now. Second Battalion Royal Fusiliers are coming on board ready for the landings tomorrow, and Gus has scrounged some extra rum rations from the mess. Us sailors'll show these boys a warm welcome, if it's the last thing we do. Although, here's hoping that it won't be....

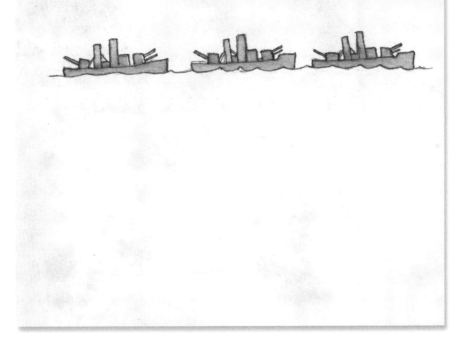

I needed to go too. The clock on the mantelpiece had chimed a warning, telling me that I was about to be late home for Sunday lunch.

"Same time next week?" Henry asked as he returned the diary to the ditty box.

"Same time next week." I nodded. "If it's not too much trouble?"

"Of course it's not, lad. You're much better company than the cabbages." And with a wink, Henry sent me on my way.

FOUR

IT HAD TAKEN ME A WHILE to fall asleep that
night. My mind was churning with thoughts of ships'
cats and crashing waves and exploding battleships. Just
before I'd dropped off, it had hazily occurred to me that
the night Henry had written the last diary entry I'd read,
he'd gone to sleep not knowing if the next day would be
his last.

When I woke up the next morning, I felt I couldn't
wait until Sunday to see Henry again, and so I threw
an excuse the editor's way, and eleven o'clock saw me
pedaling furiously in the direction of Corton.

"Back so soon?" Henry asked as I skidded to an
abrupt halt outside the railway carriage. He was leaning
on his fork, drinking tea out of a tin mug.

Ali Pasha had been moved from his snug wooden box to the wide-open space of the pen Henry had built him in the garden.

"Sorry, I know it's not a Sunday, but I just wanted to . . . no, I needed to—"

"To know what happened next?" Henry interrupted.

I nodded hopefully.

Henry passed me a spade, saying, "Well, Monday's my planting day, so if you want to know more, you'd better get digging."

I eagerly took the spade as Henry continued his story.

★ ★ ★ ★

At dawn on the twenty-fifth of April, HMS Implacable headed straight for our target, which had been code-named X Beach, plastering the cliff tops with twelve-inch shrapnel and the foreshore with six-inch shells. An armada of smaller boats, crammed with troops, followed under our stern like ducklings guided by a protective mother duck.

We kept up our bombardment of the cliffs, then our engines were thrown into a sudden reverse and the armada of smaller vessels made a final dash toward the beach.

As soon as the boats left the sheltering bulk of their mother ship, the Turks opened fire. The armada pressed on through the bullets, getting as close to the beach as possible, before their soldier cargo clambered into rowing boats manned by my Implacable shipmates. It was a daring landing, made by many brave men.

They say there's nothing you can do if a bullet has your name on it. I'd often wondered if you'd hear it coming. A fusilier I'd seen doing a Highland jig in the mess with Gus just the night before had been stretchered past me soaked in blood. Had he heard his bullet coming? And what about a "Blighty bullet"—the sort that wounds you enough to get you a ticket home, but not enough to kill you. Would it still sound like Death, or like the friendly, familiar whistle of a friend?

I didn't have to wait long to find out, because I was to be removed from Number Two Gun and the job of shelling the Turkish headlands. Instead I'd be included in the next wave of men to be sent ashore. The rest of my gun crew were coming too.

Back home, the beach was my place to find peace, to smell the salty air, to listen to the call of a gull and the whispering waves. At this beach—X Beach—there were no seagulls. You'd never hear birdsong here, only the screams of wounded and dying soldiers and the clatter of foreign fire, shells, and shrapnel. It was like running into hell itself.

I swear the sea was made of blood that day. In place of the usual flotsam of seaweed and wood, we were wading through the floating corpses of dead men and supply mules. Those poor animals—they had it bad, just like we did. Mules and horses were landed on that graveyard of a beach to transport supplies and munitions inland to the troops, but they made easy targets for the Turkish snipers. It broke this country boy's heart to see those gentle beasts fall like lambs to the slaughter.

We made a dash for the cover of the cliffs and up a zigzag track toward higher ground. Stumbling stretcher bearers picked their way down the track in the opposite direction. When we finally reached the top, we found ourselves in a landscape thickly overgrown with prickly bush and stunted, shattered trees. Wounded soldiers were strewn amongst the scrub, getting what shade they could. They reminded me of the farm workers back home who would rest in the shade of a hedge during harvest time.

Being the same height, Long John and I were put on stretcher duty. It was the job of us Implacable boys to help transport the wounded back to the beach and then out to a Cunard liner that was acting as a hospital ship. Our cargo was precious, often soldiers who were wounded so badly they were practically knocking on Death's door and begging to be let in. But the terrain was rough, and we

couldn't help but stumble
and stagger as we picked
our way over the crumbling
ravines with bullets whistling
past our ears. Every jolt must have
been agony for the heroes on our
stretchers, yet they never complained.

When night fell, we had even grislier duties
to perform. Under cover of darkness, we had to creep
across the body-strewn landscape, checking for any signs
of life.

I had to get up closer to those bodies than I cared to,
listening for faint breathing, checking for a pulse. One
boy around my age, who was caked in a grim mixture of
blood and clay and crawling with flies, seemed to awake
from a deep sleep when I touched him. He softly moaned
for his mother—and died.

But even worse than that, when random firing came from Turkish positions, we were usually forced to dive for shelter behind the bodies of those who had already fallen. As the bullets thumped into the dead man in front of me, I felt a guilt that tore my soul. He's taking another one for me, I would think.

I shed more than one tear on that battlefield, I'm not ashamed to tell you.

★ ★ ★ ★

"Those Turks were proper evil!" I cried, ramming my spade into the earth in anger.

Henry shook his head sadly. "No, son. I'm afraid it wasn't as straightforward as good and evil. Don't get me wrong, I thought exactly like you at first—and Lord only

knows it was easier to shoot guns at the enemy when I did—but then something happened to change my mind."

I stood waiting in anticipation to find out what that "something" might be, but the church bells interrupted with a distant chime, making Henry look up in surprise. "Twelve o'clock already! That means Mrs. Friston'll be back from the shops before long, and she'll be wondering why those spuds haven't been peeled yet. Go on inside, young Trevor, you might be able to squeeze in a bit more of the diary before Mrs. F. gets back and turfs you out."

So we propped up our tools and went inside.

"I'd turn straight to the entry for the twenty-fifth of May," Henry called as he headed to the kitchen. "You might just find something there that changes *your* mind too."

25th May 1915

I didn't think anything else could surprise me in this war—I was wrong! You'll never guess what happened a couple of days ago.

Since we took that high ground between X Beach and W Beach, we've been joined by other blokes who landed down the shore from us. It was like my world map had turned up in Gallipoli; there were Australians and New Zealanders, Sikhs, and Gurkha Rifles. We weren't just the British Army anymore—we were the Army of the British Empire!

We pushed through to higher ground, where the Turks retreated into their fortified fall-back positions. But we couldn't push any farther—they were just too well protected. The trenches in France must be just

RULE BRITANNIA!

like that—attack and counterattack, with no real ground gained, only casualties. "Stalemate," they call it. God help Ernie and Arthur....

Anyway, it got to a point where there were thousands of unburied bodies, with the most God-awful stink (even worse than mucking out the stables on a hot summer's day), not to mention the threat of disease for those of us still alive. So the men took matters into their own hands and raised the Red Cross flag. Of course, it was immediately riddled with bullets by the Turks. I suppose any sudden movement from the other side would make me shoot on sight too. But soon after, to our amazement, they sent a messenger with a white flag to apologize and their own Red Crescent flag was raised above their lines.

"Apologize?" I said to Henry. "But they were the enemy! How could they shoot at you one minute and apologize the next? I don't understand. . . ."

In my indignation, I'd abandoned the diary and was now standing in the doorway to the kitchen. Henry looked up from his potatoes.

"I wouldn't expect you to understand, son. You've never been to war. Funny things happen on the battlefield, things that have a habit of turning what you thought you knew right on its head."

He beckoned me over and handed me a potato and a small knife. I stood by his side, scraping the peel from the sturdy little spud as I listened in surprise to what followed.

★   ★   ★   ★

So us stretcher bearers went forward into no-man's-land— tentatively at first, I mean, everyone knew the enemy couldn't be trusted—but then we realized that the men toiling away next to us were Turkish medics and stretcher boys, who looked just as wary of us as we did of them.

We each sifted our wounded from our dead, working

in silence. It's an eerie sort of sound when you're used to screams and gunfire, that's for sure.

When the burial parties took over, we collapsed to the ground in exhausted groups, Turkish and Empire soldiers together, sitting side by side sharing our smokes and our rations.

"It's halftime in hell," Long John said as we shoved over to let two hollow-eyed Turkish lads sit beside us.

I decided I didn't want the whistle for the second half to blow. Ever.

But of course, blow it did. Polite teatime rifle shots whistled halfheartedly back and forth to begin with, neither side wanting to be the one to disturb the makeshift peace. But by three A.M. the next morning, heavy firing had started up again. I tried my hardest, but I just couldn't shake the thought that our gunfire was headed straight for the Turkish lads that I'd been huddled next to only a matter of hours before, sharing a weary smile and a cigarette. It had occurred to me that the Turkish aren't so different from us. After all, they were only defending their homeland, same as I would if a foreign army charged up the cliffs at Corton.

★ ★ ★ ★

"Told you it might change your mind," said Henry kindly. "Now, haven't you got a job to go to, young man?"

I remembered with a start that the editor would be wondering where I'd got to. Mainly because there'd have been no one to make him his morning cuppa, but nevertheless, I needed to get back to the office.

As I pedaled away from Corton that afternoon, I felt a bit ashamed. It had never really occurred to me before that there wasn't so much difference between soldiers on opposite sides in a war. My anger just seemed childish now. If Henry, who had seen and suffered so much, could think this way about the men he was fighting against, then so could I.

FIVE

THE FOLLOWING SUNDAY, I stuffed pencils in my pocket and my notepad in my satchel, yelled a rushed cheerio to Mum, and excitedly cycled off to Corton. In all the talk of ships and stretchers and no-man's-land, I'd forgotten something. An important part of the story that I was yet to uncover. The part that had put me in Henry's path to begin with. . . .

"What about Ali Pasha?" I asked as soon as we were settled on the garden bench with our usual glass of apple juice. "Where does he come into all of this?"

"I wondered when you'd ask that." Henry chuckled. "Well, as it happens, your timing is perfect. He's about to make his entrance into the story. And it's quite some entrance, let me tell you. . . ."

*   *   *   *

Long John and I had worked for several days solid with little food and water, and next to no rest. We weren't much better off than the walking wounded we were helping up and over the headland to the boats. So when the heavy fire began, it took my cloudy, sleep-deprived brain a while to realize what was happening.

Before I could dive for cover, BOOM! I was blown clean off my feet by a blast from a nearby shell and landed facedown in the muddy belly of a shallow crater.

I wiggled all my fingers and toes—all four limbs present and correct, thank God. Shots and shrapnel were pinging into the scrub all around me, so all I could do was stay still and pray that none of the bullets had my name on it.

I was alone, and I was very, very frightened.

I remember the terror wrapping itself around my heart and squeezing it tight, like a python. My tongue was dry and crunchy from taking a mouthful of dirt as I fell, and I was struggling to breathe.

But just as all hope vanished and I was about to give in to the persistent voice in my head telling me I was a goner, something rolled into my crater and hit me on the head.

A shell!

But not the kind of shell we'd become used to in Gallipoli. It was a tortoise shell. And judging by the little legs sticking out of it and wriggling in the air, it had a real, live tortoise inside!

All thoughts of lying there until Death turned up to cart me away vanished in an instant. "Stay still," I hissed at the tortoise.

It waggled a leg.

"Don't wave to them! They'll spot us!"

It waggled some more.

Henry, you idiot, I thought. You can't even speak Turkish, so you're hardly going to be able to speak Tortoise.

Reaching out slowly, gently, with the minimum of movement so as not to attract the enemy's attention, I turned the tortoise the right way up.

It immediately whipped its legs and head into its shell.

"Good idea, pal," I whispered. "Wish I could do the same."

We lay like that for ages, the tortoise and me, side by side. Somehow, having another living, breathing thing next to me in that crater calmed me right down. The python relaxed its grip on my heart, and I was able to imagine

myself far away from Gallipoli, lying in a cornfield back in Corton instead, dozing and waiting for Ma to call me in for my tea, with the summer sun warming my body.

I whispered stories of home to the tortoise. I told him all about the animals on the estate—newts and stickle-backs that swim in the ditches, slowworms that hide in the hedgerows, rabbits that bounce across the fields. I even told him about my bantam hens.

It was only when I started to tell him about the exotic fruits growing in the greenhouses at the Big House that I realized I was starving hungry. By a stroke of luck, I had some leftover rations in my pack. I reached down and felt around inside the canvas bag for the hunk of bread and the tomato that I knew were inside. What would a tortoise

eat? I had no idea, but I reckoned he'd prefer the tomato to the bread, even if it was a bit squashed.

I placed the sad-looking tomato at the head end of the shell. And waited.

The head, when it eventually emerged, was as old as Time itself. The leathery folds of skin were punctuated by two watery eyes. To me they seemed full of the tears of the entire world.

"Hello, old chap," I said. "Fancy some grub?"

The tortoise blinked soulfully at me and whipped his head back inside.

Suddenly I noticed that everything had gone quiet. Seconds later, the silence was pierced by the heavy clatter of hoofs as a dispatch rider thundered by on horseback, and I heard Gus and Long John calling my name.

"I'm all right, boys! I'm all right!" I yelled back.

I knew I couldn't take the tortoise with me. It was against ship rules, and besides, he'd be a weighty addition to my already heavy pack. So I tore some scrub from the edge of the crater and draped it over him as a makeshift shade. The sun was getting low in the sky, but the rays of heat beating down on us both were unrelenting.

"So long, fella," I said. "Thanks for keeping me company."

I wasn't wounded, so as soon as I rejoined my crew, we continued on our mission to find survivors. But as dawn rose and we made our way back to the headland with the walking wounded, we came across a dispatch rider whose horse had been shot from underneath him. He was sobbing, and his tears for his faithful animal pal made me think of the tortoise, stuck out there in that crater.

"Have a breather here, lads," I said to the others as we stopped just before the top of the headland. "I'll just check out the way ahead."

And I crept through the scrub, keeping low to the ground until I came to the spot where I'd been blown off my feet and onto my face. I peered over the rim of the crater.

"You still there?" I whispered.

A wrinkled head poked through the little haystack of grass to greet me. The tomato had gone.

"Good old boy!" I laughed. "You saved my life, staying with me in this crater, so now I'm saving yours. You're coming with me."

I carefully slipped the tortoise into my pack and returned to the resting soldiers.

It was to be the last time I would cross the headland. That night, the Implacable was transferred to other urgent duties in the Mediterranean.

I introduced our new crew member to Gus, Cornish Matt, and Long John as soon as I could. They were the only ones I trusted to keep him a secret, and each gave me his solemn oath he wouldn't tell. I think to begin with, they'd thought that smuggling a tortoise on board ship was a sure sign I'd gone and lost my marbles in that shell crater.

But before long, they'd taken to the old fella. They helped me make him a cozy home out of sawdust and newspaper in the gun well. I think the boys hoped he would bring us luck—after all, he'd cheated death once already. I'd often catch them bringing him offerings of tomatoes they'd saved from their plates on the mess deck, as if he was some sort of tiny god, watching over all of us with his beady old peepers.

They wanted to call him Gunner, but in the end, I

decided he deserved an important-sounding name, a name that would remind him of home. So I called him Ali Pasha, after the mighty ruler of the Ottoman Empire. Miss Hood would have been surprised to hear I hadn't been daydreaming in every one of her history lessons.

I'd brought Ali Pasha safely off the battlefield, and now I hoped my little Ottoman pal would see me and my mates safely back to our homeland.

★   ★   ★   ★

Henry passed me the diary as he went off to make the tea, having first nestled Ali comfortably on top of a little bed of straw in his pen. It was a throne, from where this tortoise with an imperial name could survey his garden kingdom.

I gave Ali Pasha a little bow and opened up the diary once again.

13th June 1915

Poor old Ali hasn't found his sea legs yet! We're currently giving the boys from the Italian navy a hand against the German, Austro-Hungarian, and Ottoman ships (I've not mentioned to Ali that we're fighting his own...), and when the heavy fire makes the Implacable shudder, he slips and slides across the floor of the gun pit, bouncing off the sides. Good job he's got his own armor plating.

Back at school, when I used to stare and stare at the world map on the wall, it'd never fail to amaze me just how much Italy looks like a big-heeled boot. Lately, just for the laughs, I've imagined that big boot giving Fritz's behind a good old kicking.

Implacable is currently stationed on the pointed heel of the boot, in the port of Taranto. Ali Pasha may be battered and bruised from riding the rough seas, but he's very well fed, on the freshest fruit a tortoise could wish for. Before I came to Taranto, I'd only ever seen tinned pineapple, and that was in

the larder at the Big House. But here in the port, you can buy fresh pineapples. They're encased in a hard, scaly shell, but that hides the softest, sweetest of centers. Not unlike my Ali, really.

22nd September 1915

It's been a tough month, September has. It was Ma's birthday a couple of weeks ago; how I wish I could have been there to give her a birthday hug. I'd trade anything to sit at Ma's kitchen table, even just for an hour, cuppa in hand and a slab of her famous fruitcake on a plate in front of me. I know I was desperate to see the world and all that, but I always thought I'd be able to choose when to come home. And I never imagined how much I'd miss it.

Anyway, I reckon someone, somewhere, must have known how I've been feeling and taken pity on me, as the most wonderful thing happened this afternoon. I was down at the gun with Ali, telling him all about Ma's cooking and the glorious smells that used to waft through the kitchen on baking day, when Long John came rushing in to find me. Sixty British trawlers had just arrived in port to help ferry troops and supplies, and they were tied up right by our ship. Going out on deck, I was astonished to recognize a couple of my fishing mates from Corton—lads I'd drunk with in the local pub and played cricket with on the village green!

The sight of familiar faces hundreds of miles from home was just the tonic I needed to lift my spirits. When I yelled, "On the ball, Corton!" from the deck of <u>Implacable</u>, I hope it transported them back to our sunny village green, even just for a moment.

Us gunners found some crates of beer and lowered them down to the decks of the trawlers. It was almost like we were back in the White Horse pub again, laughing and drinking together without a care in the world.

A little bit of Suffolk came to Italy today, and mighty happy it made me too.

SIX

QUITE SOME TIME had passed since my first visit
to Henry and Ali. I was desperate to write about them
for the *Journal*, and the weekends—when I would get
more for my story and see my new friends—couldn't
come soon enough.

Pedaling to Corton the following Sunday, I got to
thinking that young Henry had now been at war for more
than a year. It seemed like such a long time to be away
from friends and family—I'd never been away for more
than a night, and that was only with the Boy Scouts, just
a few miles away in Southwold. Perhaps it was time for me
to be more adventurous. After all, Henry had only been
a year or so older than I was when he'd joined the navy.

"You said once that Ali Pasha loves apples because of your time in Egypt," I said to Henry as he poured me a glass of juice. "But you haven't told me anything about that yet."

Henry grinned. "You're going to make a fine reporter one day, young Trevor—as usual, your question is perfectly timed. Egypt's exactly where the *Implacable* went next."

I'd never really paid much attention in geography lessons at school, so what I knew about Egypt was mainly to do with pharaohs and pyramids. Where would the *Implacable* have landed? I wondered. Would they have sailed on the Nile? Could battleships even sail on the Nile? I didn't want Henry to think I was stupid, but every reporter needs good, solid facts in his story, so I took a deep breath and asked my questions.

Henry pulled out his ditty box and burrowed around inside it for a short while. He drew out a large piece of yellowing paper, folded like a concertina, opened it up, and spread it out. It was a map of the world. The

very map Henry's dad had given him before he went
to war.

"Maybe this'll help you, lad. Came in mighty
handy on the *Implacable*, I can tell you. . . ." He smiled
and continued his story.

★   ★   ★   ★

I spread my map out on the floor. Long John and Gus crowded round—they loved to see where we were heading and where we'd been so far.

As the boys watched eagerly, I traced my finger along the length of the Suez Canal in Egypt. In those days, the canal was called Britain's jugular vein, because it joined the Mediterranean to the Red Sea and was the quickest naval route between Britain and her empire. The canal made it easier for the troops from our colonies to come and fight for their king—he was as much their king as he was ours, after all.

The Turks had tried to capture the canal already, and though they'd made a pretty bad go of it, there were rumors that they were building forces to have another try. If the canal was captured, supplies and reinforcements to the war in Europe would be cut off. It was absolutely vital to protect it.

So, of course, the mighty HMS Implacable, with its

equally mighty crew of sailors and one brave tortoise, sailed to Port Said, at the entrance to the Suez Canal.

Ali Pasha and I both found ourselves in our own versions of paradise. For Ali, that meant the plentiful supply of dates he now found in his food bowl and the calm of the canal waters. For me, it was the awesome fact that I had now, finally, after years of hoping and daydreaming, actually arrived in AFRICA!

I put war to one side for a while and took a stroll down memory lane in search of that young Suffolk lad who only ever dreamed of traveling the world. He was quite impressed, I can tell you.

I knew from my schoolbooks that Africa was hot and full of jungles, but I had no idea there would be so much sand. It was everywhere. Not only in the distant dunes and hills we could see from the deck of the Implacable, but right there on board, in the sandbag barricades that ringed the decks to protect us against enemy sniper fire.

When we got about halfway down the canal, we were ordered to give ourselves greater protection from the snipers by painting the entire outside of the ship the color of sand. So now we were being camouflaged by the stuff too.

As the great iron bulk of the Implacable lumbered slowly along the canal, I would often conceal Ali in the collar of my uniform and take him out on deck—there were so

many amazing sights, and I didn't want him missing any of them.

One day we watched together as hundreds of long-legged, lumpy camels got a wash- and brush-up in the canal from their riders. These men were the Bikaner Camel Corps, who were mainly Sikhs from India, but had also been joined by lads from the Australian Fourth Light Horse Regiment, who'd swapped their horses for mounts more suited to the desert.

On another trip up to the deck, I told Bible stories to Ali as we gazed at scenes of shepherds watching their flocks and family groups with mothers riding on donkeys. They were just people going about their daily business, but these sights transported me back to the Sunday school Nativity play at the Corton village chapel. As it happened, the timing couldn't have been more perfect, because by the time Implacable reached Suez at the far end of the canal, it really was Christmas.

* * * *

Christmas! The editor had sent me out to report on the primary school Nativity play for the *Journal*—it always marked the beginning of my favorite time of year, right from when I was a little boy, dressed up as a shepherd with my grandma's best tea towel on my head.

I couldn't bear the thought of being away from my family at Christmas. I'd always promised Mum that even when I became a famous reporter, I'd always be back for the turkey dinner and presents round the tree on Christmas Day.

Henry, on the other hand, didn't have that choice. He was stuck on a battleship

Henry's Christmas card home, 1915

in Africa, with no turkey or presents, and certainly no snow. Did they even celebrate Christmas in Egypt? I wasn't sure. . . .

"I bet you've had better Christmases," I said to Henry, expecting the old man to grimace at the memory of army rations and blazing sunshine instead of roast potatoes and caroling. But he threw back his head and laughed, making Ali whip himself into his shell in fright.

"Quite the opposite!" Henry chuckled. "It was one of the best Christmases I've ever had."

It seemed they did celebrate Christmas in Egypt, after all.

★ ★ ★ ★

I started my Egyptian Christmas thinking of home. We all did, I'm sure. As I clambered out of my hammock, I thought about the children back home in Corton who'd be waking up right about then too, feeling for a gift at the end of their beds. The church bells would be ringing soon, and Ma would be making a start on lunch. With so many empty chairs around the table, it'd be a small bird this year.

I was down at Number Two Gun with Ali, sending

up a silent prayer for Ernie's and Arthur's safety, when Gus burst in with a tea towel on his head and two paper crowns in his hand.

"Come on, lad," he said. "I'm a shepherd, and you and Ali can be two of the wise men. Matt and Long John are fighting over who gets to be the third wise man and who gets stuck as Mary!"

He looked ridiculous, my sun-scorched Scottish pal with his tea towel headdress, but it did the trick. My homesickness vanished, and I took the paper crowns from Gus. I put one on my head and balanced the other carefully on Ali Pasha's shell. Not quite a crown worthy of his Ottoman namesake, but Ali still looked splendid to me.

Later, on the mess deck, there were plum pudding, extra rum rations, a sing-along, and someone even read aloud from A Christmas Carol. All of us Number Two Gunners stashed away our dates for "later," which was really our code for Ali.

There were more stars than usual that night, high above the Implacable. Standing out on deck in the warm African air, Ali poking his nose out of his hiding place in my jacket, I turned to the northern horizon and looked up at the twinkling skies.

Can they see those same stars from the cliffs of Corton? I thought. And I wonder if my Christmas card arrived on time. . . .

I shifted my gaze away from the north and blinked in disbelief. There, away to the east and shining brighter than all the rest, was one single star, high in the sky above what I fancied might be the Holy Land.

I went to bed feeling peaceful that night. If only things had stayed that way.

When January came, Implacable's crew found themselves regularly sent ashore to build observation posts and extend fortifications to protect the eastern bank of the canal from attack. According to Moby, who got it from the telegraph room (as usual!), more defenses were needed because the threat from the German-led Turks had increased since Christmas.

Digging a trench was hard enough work, but things certainly weren't made any easier by the sandstorms that would whip up around you and meant you couldn't open your eyes, let alone breathe. The sand dunes that hemmed us in on all sides didn't help much either—it was like the Devil had designed them specially for Turks to hide behind so they could ambush us as we tried to carry out our duties in the swirling sand clouds. I couldn't help but feel like a sitting duck out there.

One morning, we were busy building an observation post when a sandstorm closed in on us without warning. Usually when this happened, the only sounds you could hear were the howling wind and men swearing as the sand stung their skin. But, added to that on this particular morning was the very unwelcome sound of rifle fire.

I dived for cover as soon as my brain caught up with my ears and I realized what was going on. I clamped one hand over my eyes and the other over my mouth to keep the sand out, and I sent up a prayer that none of those bullets had "Henry Friston" written on it. We all just had to hope that if we couldn't see the enemy, the enemy couldn't see us.

But the storm wasn't a long one, and as the sand began to clear, we expected it to reveal a line of Turks with their rifles pointing at us. Instead we were greeted by the sight of hundreds of camels sweeping over the dunes, spurred on by the Sikhs and the Australians of the Fourth Light Regiment. They were chasing back the retreating Turks in a great long-legged wave.

Luck was on our side that day. The enemy had almost

surrounded our observation post under cover of the sandstorm, and they'd been preparing to finish us all off.
But, despite this brush with death, we laughed and

laughed until our bellies ached—those camels looked
so comical, galloping across the dunes at full speed.
We'd never seen anything quite like it before in our lives.

*   *   *   *

I winced at Henry. "Another near miss. Must have been terrifying!"

"It was," Henry replied with a grimace. "But things were even worse at night. I remember one time . . ."

*   *   *   *

The night was well chosen. It was pitch-dark, and there was no moonlight, so we hadn't noticed the buildup of Turkish troops on the east bank of the canal. A sandstorm had masked them earlier in the day. We hadn't even realized that the Turks were there, readying themselves with their pontoons and rafts, but then they launched onto the water, and suddenly we saw them.

Thank goodness for the Sikh machine gunners lined

up along the west bank, hiding in the trenches that we'd helped dig for them. They peppered the surface of the canal like a hailstorm striking a pond—only these hailstones were made of lead. The Turks were losing badly, but they just kept coming. They poured out of the gullies along the east bank and onto rafts, trying time and again to get across but always getting driven back. They were the enemy, but we couldn't help admiring their pluck and determination.

By the time the dawn broke, the Turkish attack had crumbled. After one last failed attempt to cross, the enemy retreated into the desert, pursued by heavy fire from good old Implacable's guns.

This time, it was the Turks who were sitting ducks.

SEVEN

As I'd cycled home that afternoon, I'd tried, and failed, to imagine young Henry larking around on the beach. I just couldn't picture him splashing about in the sea and playing in the sand.

But then again, I'd been getting to know two different Henry Fristons all the time I'd been going to Corton. The Henry who pottered in his garden and tended to his cabbages was as old as my granddad, but the Henry I had been getting to know in the pages of the diary was a young man not far off my own age. I wondered if we might have been good pals, had we grown up at the same time. Would we have gone to the same school, or spent our weekends fishing at the same pond? We might even have headed off to war together. That bit didn't sound so appealing, mind you.

The week that followed was a busy one, as I found myself sent out to report on countless small local stories. I wasn't really interested in any of the things I was writing about, but I didn't have much choice but to go where the editor sent me.

By now I had nearly enough material to start the article I really wanted to write. Maybe I'd impress the editor, and he'd let me be a proper reporter.

So when Sunday finally came, I enthusiastically headed to Henry's.

"What happened next?" I began as soon as I had my juice in my hand.

"Where were we . . . ?" Henry thought hard. "Ah, yes!"

And an enormous grin broke out across his weathered face.

⋆ ⋆ ⋆ ⋆

We continued to patrol the canal for the next few months, while supply roads and a railway line were built. It was late in the day when we reached Port Said, at the top of the Suez Canal. I remember being dazzled by the sun as it bounced off of the whitewashed walls of the little houses along the bank, making them look like a row of gleaming teeth.

We hadn't even reached the port before we were surrounded by a flock of feluccas and little wooden rowing boats. Their crewmen were beaming and waving souvenirs and postcards up at the sailors who'd come out on deck. I bought a few things to take home and show my brothers— I wanted them to experience a little bit of this exotic land too. It was rotten luck for Ernie and Arthur that they'd been stuck in the trenches in France instead of getting to see the world like I had, but I knew they'd still beg me for stories about the places I'd been to.

The order to return HMS Implacable to her usual battleship-gray color came through once we'd stopped and coaled the ship. I sat beside Long John and Gus, slapping paint onto the ship's huge hull, and we chewed over the possibilities for our next posting. If Implacable was going gray again, then at least we knew that it wasn't somewhere with sand!

I decided that I'd better make sure Ali Pasha was well

stocked with fresh fruit, in case we were going to be at sea for a long time. He'd got himself a taste for dates too, so I headed straight to the market the next time I got shore leave. The sight of me staggering back on board weighed down by a pile of wooden boxes full of Ali's favorite treats couldn't fail to attract attention.

"Oi, Friston! You got enough dates there?" Moby called.

"Enough to sink a battleship!" was all I called back. I wanted my little stowaway to remain the Implacable's best-kept secret.

✦　✦　✦　✦

"What would have happened if someone had found out about Ali?" I interrupted Henry.

"Not sure, lad," Henry replied. "I was lucky enough never to find out. But I'd likely have ended up with an earful from the commanding officer. Suppose they might have thrown Ali overboard too—no unnecessary weight

allowed on the ship and all that. He can't swim, though, so I'd probably have jumped straight in after him."

My eyebrows shot up in surprise.

"Well, it's what you do for your pals, isn't it?" Henry said, and giving Ali a gentle tickle, he carried on.

*　*　*　*

So, depending on where you were on the ship and whose conversations you were earwigging, we were being sent to Norway, Russia, Holland, or France. I quite fancied Norway. I remembered its position at the very top of the world map, so it'd be the farthest north I'd ever have gone, but it was bound to be cold there, and I knew Ali wouldn't like the chilly weather.

I decided that if we were sent to Norway, I'd pinch a tea cozy from the mess to put over his shell.

But all thoughts of how to keep Ali Pasha warm vanished when, early in the morning on the twenty-second of March, the captain's orders rang out from the bridge. Our next destination was the only place none of us had even dared to hope for.

Home.

There was silence after the announcement—it lasted no more than a heartbeat, but it was as if every sound on earth had been turned off. The gulls stopped crying, the waves stopped crashing, even Implacable *herself* seemed to stop creaking. Then the sound was switched back on, and the deck exploded with whoops and cheers.

I looked around at my pals. Gus's face was split wide in a toothy grin; Long John just looked shocked, like someone had walloped him round the chops; and although he swore he hadn't for days after, Cornish Matt definitely had tears in his eyes.

Me? Well, I was desperate to get to my one pal who wouldn't have heard the captain's announcement, so while the chaos continued on deck, I slipped away to Number Two Gun to tell Ali the good news.

I crawled inside the belly of the gun pit and picked Ali up. He stared at me with his usual expectant eyes. I stared back.

"How do you fancy coming to live in England, my old chum?" I asked him. "I know it's a foreign country to you, but I promise I'll make you feel right at home."

I sat there for an hour with Ali, telling him about endless meadows he could roam in, the never-ending supply of dandelions he'd have to munch on, and the shows the dancing butterflies would put on for him out in the garden. I promised that Ma would save him the peelings when she made apple pie and that Dad would rig him up a cozy bed that didn't sway and roll from side to side. But most important of all, I promised him that he would be safe and we would be pals forever.

★ ★ ★ ★

"So that was it?" I jumped in again. "They simply sent you home?"

"There was nothing simple about it, young Trevor." Henry frowned. "There were still hundreds of miles of ocean to be crossed before we reached England, and dotted along those miles of ocean, enemy ships and U-boats were lurking goodness knows where. No, there was nothing simple about it at all."

Henry picked up his diary. He riffled through the brittle pages for a few seconds and found the entry he was looking for. He passed it back to me without a word and disappeared into the kitchen, taking Ali with him.

I read on.

28th March 1916

I've never felt more frightened during this whole bloomin' war than I do now....Facedown in a trench, firing on X Beach, under attack in a sandstorm—there's no denying that I was scared good and proper each of those times, but this is a different kind of fear. It's the kind that sends you a bit doolally.

I think it's because we're so close to being back on good old English soil that the danger seems more real than it ever has. I mean, there could be a U-boat lurking nearby at this very moment, just waiting to let loose the torpedo that will sink the Implacable....I can't bear the thought of being this close to seeing my family again but never making it home. Think I'll go down to the gun and see Ali. He always makes me feel better.

30th March 1916

I'm still here, diary. No sign of Fritz. Well, not yet, anyway....

The boys have taken to odd little superstitions lately, most of them involving Ali. We've always thought of him as our good luck charm, but it's got to the point where Gus has to give him a gentle pat every morning before he does anything else, and Long John is now convinced it's a bad omen if Ali chooses to stay inside his shell all day. Offerings saved from dinner plates keep arriving too, mainly from Cornish Matt, whose appetite is legendary. He's never left a single scrap behind at mealtimes before now.

I only wish these things would mean we were guaranteed safe passage through these treacherous waters.

2nd April 1916

We're well into the real danger zone now—the Atlantic, heading up U-boat alley to the Bay of Biscay. Not sure how much longer any of us can put up with the fear and dread of what could be lurking beneath us. No one wants any off-duty time—we just want to keep ourselves busy to avoid the waiting. And the wondering.

Even Moby's stopped telling jokes at mealtimes. Things are definitely bad.

Henry interrupted my reading as he came back in from the kitchen. I looked up, ready with an apology, but he said softly, "It's all right, lad. I just wanted you to realize that it wasn't as simple as just setting sail for home. Anyway, the story's nearly over. *Implacable*'s about to make it home in one piece."

* * * *

All my fear evaporated into the breeze, late afternoon on the eighth of April, 1916, when the mighty HMS Implacable *steamed into Plymouth Sound.*

The four of us from the Number Two Gun crew stood with our arms around one another's shoulders, singing "Rule Britannia" as we watched the sun dipping behind the hills of Devon ahead of us.

This time, Cornish Matt didn't deny the tears that were in his eyes.

I gave each lad a hug of gratitude. "That's from me and Ali," I told them. "We all made it! Through thick and thin, to hell and back, we made it! I knew Ali would bring us luck."

"Three cheers for Ali Pasha!" Gus shouted.

"Ali Pasha! Hip-hip, hooray!" we chorused in reply.

A passing officer gave us an odd look, but none of us cared one bit. We were safe and sound, and Ali Pasha's new home awaited him.

But before we could leave, we had to do ten days of spit

and polish to make the ship spotless. I scrubbed Number Two Gun turret until it was so clean you could eat your dinner off the floor—I didn't want an officer to smell a rat (or a tortoise) at this late stage!

It was bittersweet, saying good-bye. My brothers-in-arms from Number Two Gun were mates for life. A photographer took our picture as we stood at the dockside, and I slipped Ali out of my pack just in time—he was as much a part of the crew as any of us. We gave our names and addresses to the photographer, begging him to send us each a copy. We didn't know if we'd ever be together again, and we wanted to have something to remember one another by.

Then, with more hugs for me and pats for Ali, they were gone.

I sank into the seat of the train with my little Gallipoli veteran resting on my knee and gazed out of the window. I watched the green hills and woodlands rolling by and felt a really strange sensation—I think it was two and a half years of fear and tension draining away from my body and my mind. I was finally able to relax.

I closed my eyes as the train puffed away from Devon, bound for Corton and a little cottage at the end of a quiet country lane.

My journey home from the station took me past my old school. There were children playing noisily in the yard, and I stood for a moment, wondering whether that world map was still on the wall. Did any of these innocent children like to stand in front of it, dreaming about what might be waiting out there in those foreign lands? War hadn't exactly been part of my plan, but at least it had taken me to places I'd dreamed of. I knew Miss Hood would be proud.

As I walked up Corton Street and opened the gate to the cottage, I saw the curtain twitch and then the door fly open. And in that instant, I knew that nowhere else in the world would ever match up to what was here.

Home was my empire, with Ali the lord of it all.

EIGHT

HENRY SENT ME on my way that afternoon with a promise I'd come back and visit him and Ali soon. I said that of course I would, but I had something I needed to do first.

That evening, I sat down at the kitchen table with my reporter's pad and a freshly sharpened pencil and began to write. I'd made notes here and there as the weeks had passed, and even made a start on some of the article, but for the first time, I found that the words flowed right through the pencil lead and spilled straight out onto the paper. I wrote without stopping until Mum packed me off to bed.

Three days later, I had a story that I was happy with.

I went into the editor's office, placed a copy on his desk, and waited as he began to read.

He didn't say anything at first, and part of me wanted to run away back to my filing and forget about the whole thing. But then an image of Henry, Ali, and the rest of the Number Two Gun team popped into my head, and I stood firm.

The editor finished reading and looked up at me. "Not bad. Not bad at all, young Trevor," he said, nodding thoughtfully. "So that's where you've been disappearing off to on Sundays? I've seen you pedaling past my front garden on that ancient bike of yours."

And so, on page eleven of the following Friday's edition of the *Lowestoft Journal*, there was an article titled ALI PASHA—THE HERO INSIDE THE SHELL.

And best of all, it was written by Trevor Roberts, reporter.

NINE

I WENT BACK to Henry's the same afternoon the article appeared in the *Journal*. When he saw me skidding to a halt and madly waving the paper in the air, Henry put down his hoe and hurried inside the railway carriage—in search of his reading glasses, he called back to me.

I settled myself on the garden bench, and before long, Henry emerged, his glasses perched, ready, on his nose. He sat next to me and began to read my article, nodding and chuckling, and reading lines out loud to Ali.

When he'd finished, Henry looked up with a strange expression on his face and clapped me on the back. He said nothing more, but got to his feet and headed back inside, beckoning to me to follow.

In the kitchen, Henry drew out his ditty box from the old cupboard.

"Think it's time I properly showed you what's in here," he said.

As I got up to leave two hours later, Henry leaned over and pressed something into my hand. It was a ribbon of rolled-up dark blue fabric, about an inch wide. I unrolled it and took a little breath as the words HMS *Implacable* appeared, stitched in gold thread.

"My hat band," Henry said gruffly. "I want you to have it."

"I couldn't—" I began, but Henry waved away my protest.

"It's a way for me to say thank you. People have been coming to see Ali for years, but no one was ever that fussed about finding out the true story of where he came from. Not until you came along. It's been good for me to tell that story, young Trevor."

Henry walked me to the gate and shook his head yet

again at the state of my bike. As I kicked off the ground and pedaled away, he called after me.

"Told you you'd make a fine reporter!"

As each spring passed, I made sure it was my job to cover one story in particular, even after I became the editor of the *Lowestoft Journal*. I looked forward to driving—yes, I'd traded in the old bike—out to Corton, for a glass of fresh apple juice and to ask the same question of my old mate Henry Friston. . . .

"Is Ali Pasha awake?"

★ 111

WHEN I MET ALI PASHA

by Michael Foreman

During World War II, I lived above my mum's village
shop in Pakefield, just south of Lowestoft. The shop was
always crowded. As well as the locals, there were British
soldiers and sailors and American GIs in the village, all
passing through on their way to the war in Europe.

The buses from town turned around at our shop corner,
and the drivers and conductors would come in for their
tea break. Henry was one of the drivers
of the chocolate-and-cream-
colored buses, and I
remember him standing
tall among the young
warriors who were
far from home and
about to embark on
a huge and terrible

adventure. It was an adventure with which Henry was all too familiar.

There were many jokes and much laughter amid the tea and buns. I didn't understand most of the jokes at the time, and they were probably rather rude, but Henry would wink at me as if to say, "It'll make sense one day." He told me he had a son who was my age. "He likes drawing too," I remember him saying.

At the end of the war, there was no longer the threat of air raids, so I was allowed to roam farther from home. Because I knew all the bus drivers and conductors, I was able to travel free from one end of the bus route to the other, getting on and off wherever I pleased. Henry was now a ticket inspector on the buses, which certainly helped!

One day, Henry took me to his home. He lived with his wife and two sons, at the opposite end of the bus route from me—beyond the ravine and the nut wood. Home for the Friston family was a pair of wonderful old Great Eastern railway carriages.

Henry's son Don was the one who first introduced me to Ali Pasha. Ali's pen was like a mini battlefield. The earth inside was churned up by its trundling tortoise residents—all armor plated and camouflage colored, like little World War I tanks. Baby tortoises rolled around like hand grenades, but Ali himself was motionless, sitting on a bed of golden dandelions. He was definitely the Grand Pasha of all he surveyed.

Don once told me Ali would eat almost anything except tomatoes.

"He hasn't touched one since he left the ship," Henry joined in. "They probably make him seasick."

Ali Pasha's years in Henry's garden were happy and well fed, and for much of the time, he enjoyed the company of three other tortoises and an assortment of family pets, including Beano, a large ginger cat. Henry was still a green-fingered country boy at heart, growing towering rows of beans and beds full of squash, carrots, and lettuce. There were apple and pear trees, and bushes heavy with black currants and gooseberries. Every treat a tortoise could possibly desire was on offer—except, perhaps, for dates!

When it was time for Ali to hibernate, Henry would place him in a special box full of layers of sand and topped with hay, so he could bury himself inside. Henry would add newspapers and sacking to make things comfortable, and there, safe and secure, he slept every winter away.

And then, when the first spring blooms opened their faces to the sunshine, Ali Pasha would wake from hibernation. Like the arrival of the new season, Ali Pasha was, in Henry's words, "regular as dandelion clockwork."

ALI PASHA, SUPERSTAR!

As if it weren't enough to be a war hero, Ali Pasha went from being a local personality to a national and then international celebrity, appearing in newspapers and on television around the world.

In 1968, the *News of the World* newspaper published an article about Ali and Henry. The story traveled the globe, and when it appeared in the *Age* newspaper in Melbourne, Australia, the Tail-Waggers' Club of Australia made Ali Pasha an honorary member.

The *Times* featured Ali in a major article in 1986, as did a German newspaper, *Die Aktuelle*. That same year also saw his television debut, on the BBC's *Blue Peter*, where he was awarded a coveted Blue Peter badge.

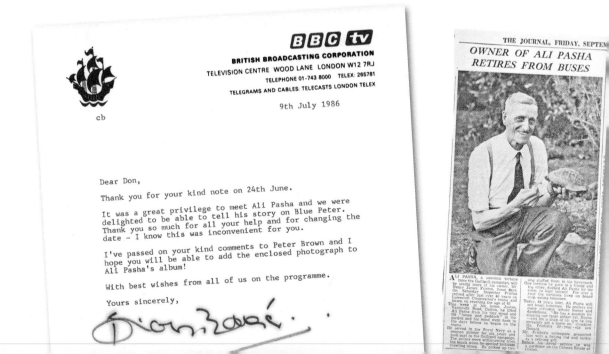

May 24-30, 1986

SATURDAY

A weekly guide
to leisure, entertainment
and the arts

Suresh Karadia

A Great War survivor of shot and shell

A grand old Turkish warrior, who was taken prisoner at Gallipoli in 191...

DIARY OF A WAR VETERAN

Extracts from the diary of ... I found myself doing ...

ALI COMES OUT OF HIS SHELL

ALI PASHA is a real little
hard case.
The shell-shocked

e Tail-Waggers' Club

Under the auspices of the R.S.P.C.A.

"I Help My Pals"

112 W...

Aug...

Mr. Henry Friston
Corton
Suffolk
England.

Dear Mr. Friston,

The Melbourne "Age" told t...
Ali Pasha, and I, as Tail-Wagger-...
the Tail-Waggers' Club in Austra...
to ask you to accept an honorary...
ship of the Club for your most u...

Of course, there are many pet Tortoises...
but Ali Pasha will be the first to become a
member of this Club, the motto of which is,
"I Help My Pals". I guess, that Ali has helped
you in many ways, particularly in the act of
remembering the heroism of Gallipoli. I myself,
am an ex serviceman, serving in the R.A.A.F
during the second War.

Thank you, on behalf of all diggers, for
your expression of admiration of our significanc...
of Anzac Day - it is indeed inspiring to watch
the men of two great Wars marching in this uniqu...
get together of warriors. Not only men - nursin...
Sisters and Voluntary Aides also.

Will you "invest" Ali Pasha on my behalf...
His badge and certificate of membership are en...
The unusualness of your Tortoise is, that he h...
from Gallipoli and the fact that a soldier ami...
all the horror of War, thought to care for a c...
so unlikely as a Tortoise. We, here in Austra...
agree "there will always be an England - and ...
Australia" while the spirit of Anzac keeps al...

So here's to Ali Pasha -
Yours most sincerely,

TAIL-WAGGER-IN-...

Member's Certificate

"ALI PASHA"

OWNED BY HENRY FRISTON
MADE HONORARY LIFE MEMBER OF THE

TAIL-WAGGERS' CLUB

and in this way is "Helping his Pals"

All profits go to
The Royal Society for the Prevention
of Cruelty to Animals,
112 Wellington Pde., East Melbourne
41-4138

Tail-Wagger-in-C...

Date 16th August 196...

...e is plenty of juicy
dandelion, lettuce and
cucumber. But he prefers
people to other tortoises
and will aggressively chase
his fellows off.

AFTERWORD

After Henry Friston died, aged eighty-three, Don looked after Ali. The tortoise soldiered on for another ten years before he too passed away, at over one hundred years old.

The *Times* and the *Daily Telegraph* both paid their respects to "the Tortoise Veteran of Gallipoli."

Henry's railway carriage home

Henry in his bus driver's coat with son Peter and dog Ruffles

Scouts off to camp on the tram, with Henry as conductor

Henry in his tram conductor's uniform

Sea Wall bus with Henry as driver, 1932